# Zip, Zip... HOMEWORK

Nancy
Poydar

Holiday House / New York

Text and illustrations copyright © 2008 by Nancy Poydar
All Rights Reserved
Printed and Bound in Malaysia
The art for this book was created in gouache and pencil.
The text typeface is Happy.
www.holidayhouse.com
First Edition
1 2 3 4 5 6 7 8 9 10

Library of Congress Cataloging-in-Publication Data
Poydar, Nancy.
Zip, zip . . . homework / by Nancy Poydar. — 1st ed.
p. cm.
Summary: Violet has a great new backpack with wheels and
zippers, but when she forgets to take home her homework and tells
a lie to cover it up, the teacher gives her an even harder assignment.
ISBN 978-0-8234-2090-2 (hardcover)
[1. Backpacks—Fiction. 2. Homework—Fiction. 3. Truth—Fiction.
4. Schools—Fiction.] I. Title.
PZ7.P8846Zi 2008
[E]—dc22
2007003258

For Felix and Billy
Let the reading begin.

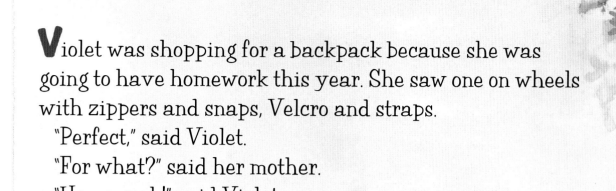

**V**iolet was shopping for a backpack because she was going to have homework this year. She saw one on wheels with zippers and snaps, Velcro and straps.

"Perfect," said Violet.

"For what?" said her mother.

"Homework!" said Violet.

Every day she rolled her pack to school just in case she got homework.

The older kids talked about homework.

"Ms. Patience gives tons of homework," said Sky.

"Be sure you don't lose it!" warned Jim.

Violet wasn't worried one bit!

Squeak! Squeak!

At her house, Violet had a place all ready to do homework.
She liked to practice filling her pack. She would *zip*, *snap*,
*stick*, and *click* until her mother called,

"Violet, you'll wear that pack out!"

Sometimes she would pretend to be Ms. Patience and herself at the same time.

"Homework not done?"
she'd say in a big voice.

"Yes it is," she would say
in a tiny voice.

"It's a good thing you didn't
lose it, young lady."

"I kept it in this pack."

Then Ms. Patience would exclaim, "Violet, that's the most beautiful pack I've ever seen!"

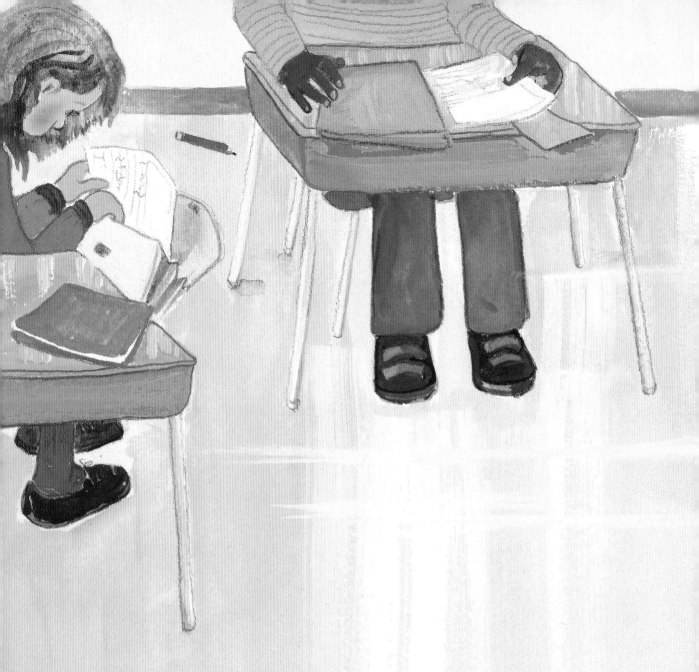

Finally Ms. Patience said she had a paper for everyone
to do at home.

"Ms. Patience, is it homework?" asked Violet.

"Yes, Violet," said Ms. Patience.

Violet was thrilled. She tried to decide which pack pocket
to put it in.

*Briiiiing* went the dismissal bell.

Violet closed up her pack. *Zip, stick, click, snap.* It was ready for rolling home.

"That's quite a pack, Violet," said Ms. Patience.

"It's for homework," said Violet.

Squeak
squeak
squeak

"I have tons of homework," hollered Violet when she got home.
"Everyone has to be quiet while I work!"
  After a homework snack, she went to get her paper.

*Ziiip. No. Ziiip.*

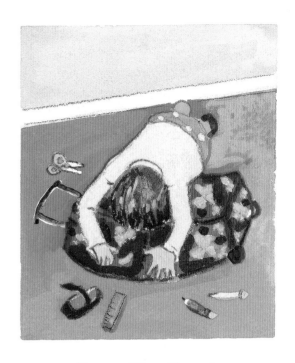

*Riiip. No. Stiick.*

*Unclick. No. Click.*
*Unsnap. No. Snap.*

No homework paper!

"My homework got lost," she imagined telling Ms. Patience in a tiny voice.

"**WHAT?**" Ms. Patience would be horrified.

Violet did not have to pretend to be scared.

"**Look again, young lady!**" Ms. Patience would not be patient.

*Ziiip*, no. *Riiip*, no. *Unclick*, no. *Unsnap*, no.

Violet's homework was not there, so she closed her pack for good.

"Sounds like you finished your homework!" called her father.

"I just put it in my pack," called Violet, because she didn't want to talk about it.

At bedtime her mother said, "That rolling pack is perfect! Sweet dreams."

But sweet dreams didn't come to Violet.
Instead she had *ziiipping*, *riiipping*, *cliiicking*,
and *snaaapping* dreams all night long.

The next day Violet walked to school slowly.
"The homework wasn't too bad," said Tom.
"It was a snap," said Violet.
"It didn't take too long," said Ali.
"I zipped right through it," said Violet.
"I wish I had a pack like that," said Kerry.
 Not me, thought Violet.

At school Ms. Patience collected their homework.
Violet fiddled with her pack, *ziiip, rip* . . .
Ms. Patience said, "What are you doing, Violet?"
Violet mumbled, "Getting my homework. I finished it
and put it in a pack pocket somewhere. . . ."

"Are you looking for this?" Ms. Patience asked. "I found it under your desk after school."

"Oh," said Violet in a tiny voice.

"We'll need to talk at recess time," said Ms. Patience.

When recess time came, Ms. Patience said, "Violet, the truth is more important than homework, you know."

Violet never imagined Ms. Patience saying *that*.

"I kept the truth zipped up," said Violet.

"But did you lose the truth?" asked Ms. Patience.

"No," said Violet, and she told Ms. Patience the truth.

Violet did her homework right then. It was a snap. Ms. Patience didn't give her a happy face sticker, but she did give her a special homework assignment.

That night Violet told her parents the truth. It was her special homework assignment, and it was harder than the homework she didn't do the night before.

Her mother and father did not have happy faces, but Violet knew they hadn't lost them.

Then Violet got some yarn and tied
one piece onto her pack. "Perfect," she said.
"For what?" asked her father.
"For finding the homework pocket,"
said Violet.

The next time Ms. Patience handed out homework, Violet knew just where to put it in her pack. *Zip. Zip!*

*Squeak...squeak...riiip...ziiip...click... ziiip...snap* went all the new rolling packs in Ms. Patience's room.

Violet got out the homework-pocket yarn. *Sniiip sniiip.*